From Dawn till Dusk

Natalie Kinsey-Warnock
Illustrated by Mary Azarian

HOUGHTON MIFFLIN COMPANY
BOSTON

MY BROTHERS AND SISTER AND I grew up on a farm of steep, wooded hills and fields with rocks as big as your head.

There was work enough on that farm to keep us busy all year long from dawn till dusk.

On winter nights, as the wind whistled 'round the house and snow piled up against the windows, our mother told stories of how our Scottish ancestors left their rocky farms to journey to America for a better life. We thought of the rocks here, of Vermont's long, bitter winters, and of the hundreds of trees that had to be cut down to make a farm, and my brothers would say, "Why'd they ever move *here?*" Then they'd argue about where they wanted to move to when they grew up.

"Think of all the things you'd miss," I told them.

"Miss?" they said. "What would we miss?"

"Well ... sugaring," I said, and my brothers hooted.

"Who'd miss sugaring?"

Spring came late to Vermont's Northeast Kingdom, and it began with sugaring.

Dad bored holes in the maple trees. My brothers and I and seven cousins tapped an iron spout into each hole and hung buckets from those spouts. We tapped thousands of trees, and when the sap ran we scurried to gather it, pour it into tanks, and haul it to the sugarhouse.

"Remember how our hands and feet get so cold we can't feel them?" my brothers asked, and I did remember that bone-chilling cold.

But I thought of how we warmed up in the sugarhouse, where my uncle Bob was boiling sap into amber maple syrup. The air was filled with steam and the smell of hot syrup.

Sometimes my aunt Eunice or my mother boiled a kettle of syrup to make sugar-on-snow. We gobbled down the sweet maple candy with sour pickles and my aunt's raised doughnuts. My brothers and cousins ate plenty of those.

"Eunice does make good doughnuts," my brothers agreed. "But what about mud season? How could you miss that?"

April was mud season. Cars and trucks sank up to their running boards, and farmers kept busy pulling them out. They never charged anything; that's just what neighbors did.

We couldn't help but track mud everywhere, and my mother threw up her hands at trying to keep the floor clean.

But I made mud pies with my cousins, and we rode our bicycles with our barn boots on, splashing through the puddles, and came home so mud-spattered you couldn't tell us apart.

When the mud dried and the grass began to grow, it was time to build fence. My oldest brother drove the iron bar deep into the ground. I held the peeled cedar posts in the holes while my father pounded them in with the post maul, and we strung electric wire around the field to hold in the cows. There were miles of fence to build.

Some evenings, though, there was time to dig worms and go fishing at the pond. We caught buckets of hornpout and fried them for supper with dandelion greens and fiddleheads.

Each spring, frost pushed rocks to the surface, rocks that would bend and break machinery if left in the field. After my father plowed the fields, we had to pick stone. Picking stone was the job we hated most. Each field had hundreds—no, thousands—of stones. Stones as far as the eye could see—more stones than could ever be picked. But we picked them.

"Even *you* wouldn't miss picking stone," my brothers said.

But killdeer always came skittering across the fields as we picked, and swallows wheeled in the air. Sometimes, when we whistled to the meadowlarks, they answered us back.

Summer meant long, hot days of haying.

My father sharpened the knives on the cutter bar and mowed the tall grass. After the grass dried in the sun and wind, my brothers raked it, then baled it.

My mother drove the tractor. My brothers and I threw the bales onto the wagon, and my sister stacked them, crisscrossing the layers so the load would hold together back to the barn.

Hay chaff stuck to our sweaty bodies, itching like a thousand mosquito bites.

But when the last bale from the field was in the barn, we drove a mile to Hartwell Pond. Even past dark, our feet knew the path, and that black, cold water washed away the dirt, chaff, and tiredness of the day. As we swam, Mother called out our names every so often, to keep track of us.

Some nights, my cousins and I slept in the hay, but we were too scared to sleep. Emily and Earl were especially good at telling ghost stories.

Summer brought berries. My mother, sister, and I picked gallons of wild strawberries, raspberries, gooseberries, and currants. Even though I loved berries, I wanted to be with my brothers instead.

My brothers didn't like me tagging along all the time, but sometimes they let me play baseball with them. I ran through the hard stubble of the hayfields to catch fly balls, playing past dark when the only lights were fireflies and the only sounds were the crack of the bat and the smack of the grass-stained ball in my brothers' well-oiled gloves.

"You'd miss that," I told them, and I could see in their eyes that they remembered too. For once they just nodded and didn't say anything.

Mornings and evenings, we got the cows and drove them to the barn for milking.

If a cow was missing, we knew she'd had her calf and hidden it. It might take hours to find her, and when we did, we carried the calf home on our shoulders.

It was my job to feed the calves. For the first few weeks I fed them from a bottle, but then I had to teach them to drink out of a pail. First I got them sucking on my fingers, then slowly drew their heads down into the pail. The first time their noses went under the milk, they snorted and jerked their heads out, flinging milk everywhere.

While Dad was milking, my sister, brothers, and I fed the cows grain and hay. We shoveled the manure from the gutters and put fresh sawdust bedding under each cow.

"I wouldn't miss milking," one brother said. "I wouldn't miss shoveling manure," said another.

But I thought of the haymow and how we looked for new kittens that the mother cats had hidden. Sometimes we found them, soft yellow, black, and gray bundles with their eyes not yet open and not yet wild. We gave them names like Sarsaparilla, Fraidy Cat, and Ralph, and they kept the barn free of mice.

In the fields and garden, we raced to stay ahead of the weeds. We hilled the potatoes, hoed the corn, and thinned the carrots. The summer my youngest brother was born, my mother couldn't bend very easily, so it was my job to tend the garden. The garden was especially weedy that year.

    None of us liked weeding . . .

but we loved the first meals of fresh vegetables: new peas and potatoes, tomatoes and corn. We ate plates and plates of fresh lettuce and cucumbers with vinegar and salt. Mother said I'd eat anything with vinegar and salt.

In September, we were back at school.

The cooler nights of fall brought out the bright color of the maple trees—red and orange and gold. Weren't we lucky to be living in the most beautiful place in the world?

My father cut corn, and we harvested all the food we'd grown. We dug potatoes, husked corn, and hauled wheelbarrows full of squash, cucumbers, carrots, and beets back to the house. My mother spent weeks canning, pickling, and freezing vegetables for the winter ahead.

We loved picking apples. I climbed the trees to shake down McIntosh, Duchess, and Northern Spy. We stuffed them into bags and carried them to the cider press. The apples rumbled down into the grinder, and the juice ran out in a clear, golden stream, tart and sweet at the same time. The hornets liked it as much as we did.

Sundays were a day of rest.

Milking had to be done, of course, but no other work. We bathed and dressed in our best clothes and drove the seven miles to church, no matter what the weather.

My brothers and cousins didn't like going to church, and we weren't allowed to go fishing on Sundays, or play cards or baseball.

But some Sunday afternoons, especially in the fall, we went for family drives. Where we lived, every road was a back road and we explored them all, finding old cellarholes and cemeteries with the names of our ancestors carved in the stones.

We cut wood for the coming winter. My father said wood warmed you three times: once when you cut it, twice when you split it, and three times when you burned it.

Snow came in October and sometimes stayed until June. Winter meant short days and cold temperatures, even down to fifty degrees below zero. Cars and tractors wouldn't start, and water pipes froze.

"Wouldn't you like to live where you didn't have seven months of winter?" my brothers asked.

But I knew how they loved to dig tunnels and build snow forts, and we had terrific snowball fights. And we all tried to fly, my brothers and cousins and me. We jumped out of trees, off silos and hay wagons. My brothers and I even skied off the barn roof.

The year ended with four Christmases: one at school, one at home, one at church, and one at my grandmother's with her eight children and thirty-two grandchildren.

In the church pageant, I was always an angel. Bigger kids got to be Joseph or Mary or shepherds or wise men, but we smaller kids were angels. We wore slips and carried candles, until the year Karen caught Debbie's hair on fire. The next Christmas, we carried flashlights.

At my grandmother's house, the little kids ate in one room, the big kids in another, and the adults in another. My cousins and I couldn't wait to eat with the big kids, and when I got older I did sit at the big kids' table. I still do.

A few cousins moved away, to New York and Michigan and even one to Africa, but my sister, brothers, and I, and most of my cousins, are still here, sugaring and haying and cutting wood. We also cross-country ski and canoe and gather together to eat, laugh, and tell stories. And no one talks about leaving.

Family photo taken at Uncle Bob and Aunt Eunice's on our way home from church, summer 1958. Pictured are my parents, Fred and Louise Kinsey, and my brothers and sister (from left to right) Blaine, Helen, me, and Leland (our youngest brother, Kyle, wouldn't be born until 1967).

Playing baseball up in the barn with my two older brothers: Leland (holding bat) and Blaine (with ball and glove).

Sledding off the barn roof: me, Helen, Leland, and Blaine.

Bob is my father's brother and Eunice is my mother's sister, so this is our family of double cousins. Back row (from left to right): Erwin, Jennie, Bob, Eunice, Everett. Front row: Jeffrey, Valerie, and the twins, Emily and Earl.

Mary Azarian also grew up on a farm—in Virginia, where her grandfather kept chickens and her uncle raised a large market garden. In the early 1960s, she and her husband moved to a small hill farm in Vermont. Their three sons were born there, and they farmed with horses and oxen, kept a milk cow, and had a large vegetable garden. In the spring, they made maple syrup, providing the bulk of their farm income.

Mary on her pony named Patsy. Springfield, Virginia, 1947.

Grandpa Hatch feeding his chickens. Springfield, Virginia, 1947.

Haying in Cabot, Vermont, 1967.

To my dozens of cousins, but especially to my uncle Bob and aunt Eunice and my seven double cousins: Jennie, Everett, Erwin, Earl, Emily, Jeffrey, and Valerie
—N.K.-W.

To Ethan, Jesse, and Tim—my Vermont farm boys
—M.A.

Text copyright © 2002 by Natalie Kinsey-Warnock
Illustrations copyright © 2002 by Mary Azarian

www.houghtonmifflinbooks.com

The text of this book is set in Monotype Italian Oldstyle.
The illustrations are woodcuts, hand tinted with watercolors.

Library of Congress Cataloging-in-Publication Data

Kinsey-Warnock, Natalie.
From dawn till dusk /Natalie Kinsey-Warnock ;
illustrated by Mary Azarian.
p. cm.
Summary: Reminiscences about the experiences a girl shared with
her family throughout the various seasons on their Vermont farm.
HC ISBN 0-618-18655-7 PA ISBN 0-618-73750-2
[1. Farm life—Vermont—Fiction. 2. Family life—Vermont—Fiction.
3. Seasons—Fiction. 4. Vermont—Fiction.] I. Azarian, Mary, ill. II. Title.
PZ7.K6293 Fr 2002
[E]—dc21
2002000411

HC ISBN-13: 978-0-618-18655-6
PA ISBN-13: 978-0-618-73750-5

Manufactured in Singapore
TWP 10 9 8 7 6 5 4 3 2